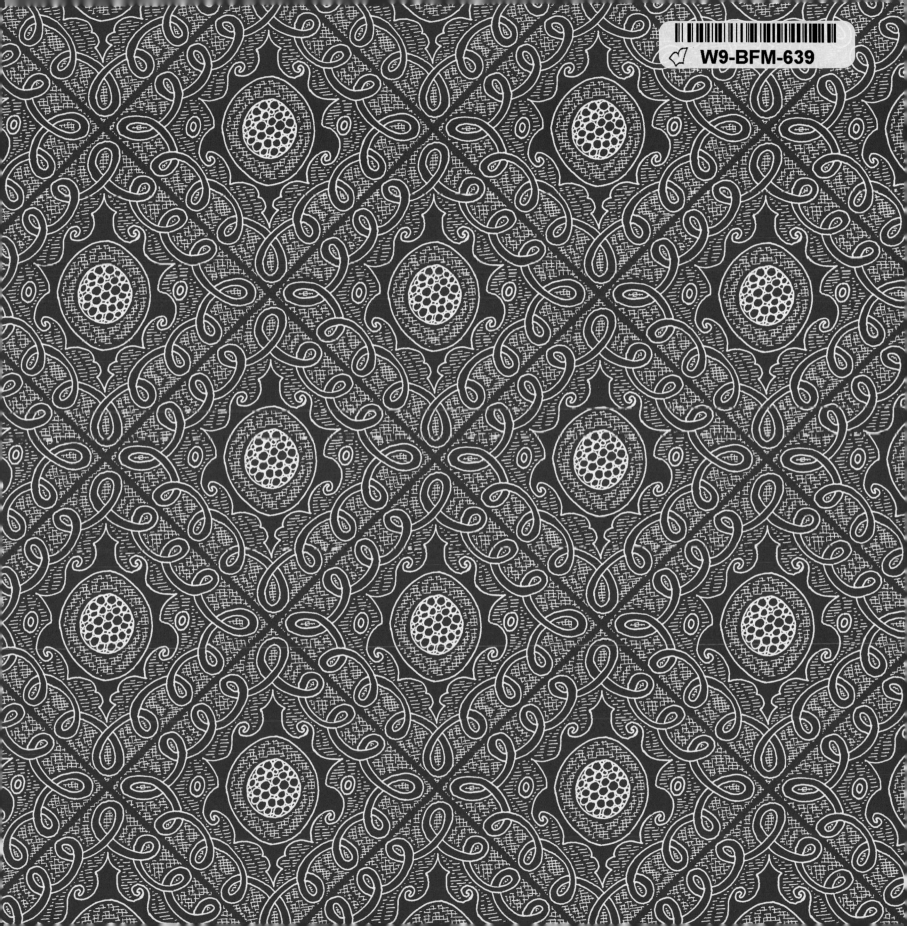

Happy 1st B-day

To: Lucy

♡ whid & La

2017

The full-color art was prepared with watercolor on photocopied drawings.

The text type is Latienne.

Library of Congress Cataloging-in-Publication Data

Bergman, Mara.

Yum yum!: what fun! / by Mara Bergman ; illustrations by Nick Maland.

p. cm.

"Greenwillow Books."

Summary: A series of animals sneaks into the house, looking for something to eat.

ISBN 978-0-06-168860-7 (trade bdg.)

[1. Animals—Fiction.] I. Maland, Nick, ill. II. Title.

PZ7.B452225Yu 2009   [E]—dc22   2008012640

First Edition 10 9 8 7 6 5 4 3 2 1

 Greenwillow Books

YUM, YUM! What Fun!

Written by **Mara Bergman**   Illustrated by **Nick Maland**

Greenwillow Books *An Imprint of HarperCollinsPublishers*

CREAK,
CRACK,

CREAK,
CRACK.

Did anyone see who crept through the window,
long and lean and scaly and green?

Not Katie or James or
their little dog Harry.

CLUMP,

STUMP,

Did anyone see
    who slumped through the window,
    with wobbly lips
        and wiggly hips
        and a lumpety bump
        of a hump?

Not Katie or James
or their little dog Harry.

Hisssssssssssssss, swissssssssshhhhh, hisssssssss, swisssssshhh.

Did anyone see
   who slid through the window,
   slippery as soap
      and skinny as rope?

Not Katie or James or
their little dog Harry.

TRIT,
TROT,

TRIT,
TROT.

Did anyone see
    who tripped through the window,
    neighing and braying
        and searching for hay?

Not Katie or James or
their little dog Harry.

SNAP!

EVERYONE saw
who stormed through the window,
rough and ready,
big and heavy,
hairy and just
a little bit scary—
even Katie and James
and their little dog Harry!

HUMPH!

sssssssssssssssssss!

NEIGH!

EEEEEEEEEEEEK!

"It's a bear!" someone squeaked.

What was it after?
Something to eat?
A crocodile, a camel?
A snake or a horse?

KATIE AND JAMES AND THEIR LITTLE DOG HARRY, OF COURSE!

But the bear wanted bread,
at least that's what he said.

"YUM, YUM!"

Then everyone else wanted some—
with butter and marmalade, honey and jam,
eggs, cheese, salami, bananas, and ham . . .

But did they EVER go home?
Well, yes, they certainly did.

The camel left first, then the horse, croc, and snake.
The big bear went last; he was searching for . . .

CAKE!

And when they were gone
a great relief it was, too,
for Katie and James
and their little dog Harry.

(PHEW!)